The Boxcar Children Mysteries

THE MYSTERY OF THE MUMMY'S CURSE

created by
GERTRUDE CHANDLER WARNER

Illustrated by Hodges Soileau

SCHOLASTIC INC.
New York Toronto London Auckland Sydney
New Delhi Mexico City Hong Kong Buenos Aires

ISBN 0-439-35371-8

12 11 10 9 8 7 6 5   7/0

Printed in the U.S.A.   40
First Scholastic printing, May 2002

Contents

CHAPTER 1

A Secret at the Museum

"Wow, look over there! Is that a T-rex?" Six-year-old Benny Alden was pointing toward a giant skull with long, pointed teeth.

"Yes, Benny, I think it is," said his twelve-year-old sister, Jessie.

"Cool," said their sister Violet, who was ten. She came over for a closer look.

"And look at this triceratops skull," said Henry, their fourteen-year-old brother. He pointed to another skull with horns coming out of the top.

The children were visiting the Dinosaur Room at the Greenfield Museum. "I always loved this room when I was a kid," said their grandfather, James Alden.

The children had lived with their grandfather ever since their parents died. At first, afraid that he would be mean to them, the children had run away. They had lived in an old boxcar they'd found in the woods. But once they met their grandfather, they found that he was a kind man, and they came to live in his large house. They had been happy there ever since. Grandfather had even moved the boxcar to their backyard, so the children could play in it. And today they were visiting the local museum.

When the Aldens had seen all the dinosaur bones, Grandfather asked what they would like to do next.

"Have lunch!" cried Benny.

"We should have guessed," said Jessie. "It's been at least an hour since breakfast."

Everyone laughed. They knew Benny was always hungry.

"Maybe soon, Benny," Grandfather said. "But first there's someone I'd like you to meet." He led them down the hall to a door that read, MUSEUM CURATOR.

"Come in," called a voice inside, after they knocked.

Grandfather pushed open the door to reveal a small office where a dark-haired man was sitting behind a desk. The man was tall and thin with a friendly smile on his face. He stood up when he saw the Aldens and came over to say hello.

"James Alden!" the man said, reaching out to shake Grandfather's hand. "My father told me you still lived in Greenfield."

"It's good to see you, Pete," Mr. Alden said. "Children, this is Peter Miller. I've known him since he was born. His father is an old friend of mine. When he told me Pete had come to the museum to work as the curator, I had to stop by and say hello."

"And these must be your grandchildren," said Mr. Miller. "Don't tell me — the tall one is Henry, Jessie is over here, Violet has the purple shirt on, and this must be Benny."

Benny grinned. "You got it!"

"Would you like to join us for some lunch, Mr. Miller?" Henry asked.

"That sounds great," Pete said. "But please don't call me 'Mr. Miller.' I'm Pete."

"When did you become the curator here?" Grandfather asked as they walked down the hallway to the museum café.

"And what is a cur — what's that word again?" Benny asked.

"A cu-ra-tor," Pete said slowly. "It's the person at the museum who puts together the exhibits."

"Which exhibits did you put together?" asked Jessie.

"I'm working on my first one," Pete said. "It's very exciting."

"What's it about?" Violet asked.

Before Pete could answer, Benny called out, "Hey, look! A mummy!" Everyone turned to see where Benny was pointing. On the wall was a poster of an Egyptian mummy.

"That answers Violet's question," Pete said. "That poster is for our new exhibit about ancient Egypt. It's called 'Enter the Mummy's Tomb.' "

"Will there really be a mummy?" Benny wanted to know.

"You bet," Pete said as they reached the café. "Let's get some lunch and I'll tell you all about it."

A few minutes later, Pete and the Aldens sat down to eat. The children had chosen sandwiches and fruit, and the two men were having soup.

But for once, Benny wasn't interested in food. "Please tell us about the mummy," he begged Pete.

Pete began speaking in a low voice. "The director of the museum wants to keep the details of the exhibit a secret," he explained. "But I don't think anyone will hear me."

"Why are you keeping it a secret?" Jessie asked quietly.

"Well, it's not really a secret," Pete said. "We've announced the exhibit in the newspapers and put up posters around town. But this is the biggest exhibit ever to come to the Greenfield Museum. We want to make sure we've got it all set up perfectly before we let out any details."

"You must know a lot about Egypt if you made an exhibit about it," Benny said.

"Actually, the exhibit was put together by the Egyptian Museum," Pete said. "We're renting it from them. Museums often share exhibits. We've also hired an expert on Egypt to help set it up."

Pete paused to eat a spoonful of his soup. Henry looked around and noticed that a young woman sitting near them had stopped eating her lunch and was watching them closely. Henry wondered why.

"Do you know what a mummy is?" Pete asked Benny.

"It's a dead person wrapped in bandages, right?" Benny said.

"That's about right," Pete said. "In ancient Egypt, they believed that when a person died they would still need their body. So they figured out a way to preserve it. They did such a good job that some mummies have lasted for thousands of years."

"Wow, that's old!" Benny said in an awed voice.

"Some mummies, especially the mummies of kings, are decorated with beautiful masks and fancy painted coffins. Some have gold and jewels on them. But our mummy isn't quite that fancy. Our exhibit will also show lots of things Egyptian people made and used thousands of years ago."

Henry was very interested in the exhibit. But he couldn't help thinking that someone else seemed to be, too. The woman sitting nearby was still watching them. She had finished eating, but she continued to sit at her table looking toward the Aldens. Henry wondered if she could hear what they were saying.

Then Henry noticed something strange.

The woman had her hands under the table. She seemed to be holding something in her lap. Henry couldn't see what it was. Why would she be hiding something under the table?

When they'd all finished their lunches, Pete said, "I'd better get back to my office."

"When did you say the exhibit opened?" Jessie asked.

"In two weeks," Pete said, standing up.

"I don't know if I can wait that long!" cried Benny.

Pete smiled and his eyes sparkled. In a hushed voice he said, "The mummy is being delivered this afternoon. Would you like to see it?"

Without a moment's pause, all four children cried, "Yes!"

Pete and Grandfather laughed. "I have to get back to my office," Grandfather said, "but the kids can walk home later without me."

"Then let's go," Pete said.

As the children said good-bye to Grandfather and left with Pete, Henry looked back at the young woman sitting near them. For the first time, she noticed Henry looking at her. She quickly stuffed whatever she was holding into a large, orange bag at her feet. Pete had said the details of the exhibit were supposed to be a secret. Had the woman overheard? Had she been listening to their conversation? And what had she put into her bag?

As Pete led the Aldens back down the hall, a voice called out, "Pete?"

Pete turned and stepped into the office next to his. "Yes, Reginald?" he said, motioning for the children to follow him.

Sitting behind a desk was a man about Grandfather's age. Behind him were a large Egyptian painting and a bookcase. Crowded in with the books were Egyptian pots and sculptures.

"Has the mummy arrived?" the man asked.

"I was just going to check now," Pete said. "These are the grandchildren of my father's good friend." Then he turned to the Aldens. "This is the director of the museum, Dr. Reginald Snood."

Pete turned back to Dr. Snood, who was putting papers into his briefcase. "I'm bringing the kids to see the mummy, if you'd like to join us. . . ."

Dr. Snood didn't seem to hear what Pete had said. He seemed to be deep in thought for a moment. Then he shook his head and seemed to see the Aldens for the first time. "I hope these children know not to touch anything," Dr. Snood said. "In my opinion, children don't belong in museums."

"They're very well behaved," Pete assured him.

"We're very excited to 'Enter the Mummy's Tomb,' " Jessie said.

"I just hope we haven't taken on more than we can handle with that exhibit," Dr. Snood said, snapping his briefcase shut and standing up.

"It looks like you're interested in Egypt," Henry said, motioning toward the artwork all around them.

"Dr. Snood is one of the world's leading Egyptologists," Pete told them. "That means he's an expert on ancient Egypt. He collects all kinds of—"

"That was years ago," Dr. Snood said, cutting Pete off, "before I became the director here. Now I have a museum to run. I have to make sure we don't waste all our time and money on one exhibit."

"This was expensive, but it will be such a hit," Pete insisted. "Sam Dickerson, the Egyptologist we've hired, will handle all the details."

"We're paying Dr. Dickerson too much," Dr. Snood said sharply. "We should have let the Carson City Museum have this exhibit."

Pete took a deep breath. "Well, anyway, as I mentioned before, we're expecting the mummy to be delivered soon. Would you like to come see it?"

A strange look passed over Dr. Snood's

face again. Then he seemed to change his mind about something. "No, I can't . . ." he said. "I have . . . a meeting. This is a very busy week." And he quickly left the office.

The Aldens looked at each other. Why had Dr. Snood left so quickly?

After a moment, Benny said quietly, "I don't think he likes us."

Pete laughed. "He takes a little getting used to. He has a very big job, running the museum. He has to make sure the museum has enough money to pay for all the exhibits and the people who work here."

They walked slowly out of Dr. Snood's office and headed down the hall.

"What did he mean about the Carson City Museum?" Henry asked.

"When the Egyptian Museum offered to rent out this exhibit, the Carson City Museum wanted it," Pete told the children. "But the Egyptian Museum decided to send it here instead. The director of the Carson City Museum was very upset."

"I didn't know museums fight over their exhibits," said Jessie.

"Sometimes they do," Pete said. He looked at his watch. "Come on, we've got a mummy to meet."

Pete led the children upstairs and down a long hallway to a room filled with tables and cardboard boxes. There was a desk in one corner with a computer on it and several neat stacks of papers and notecards. "This is the prep or 'preparation' room," Pete said.

At the back of the room were two large crates. Next to the crates stood two women. One was tall with lots of curly red hair. The other woman was short and blond.

"Dr. Dickerson," Pete said, walking to the back of the room and putting out his hand to the tall, redheaded woman.

"But, but — I thought you said *Sam* Dickerson," Benny said.

Dr. Dickerson threw back her head and laughed loudly. "That happens all the time. My real name is Samantha. But people call me Sam."

"I hope you don't mind my bringing some mummy hunters along," Pete said.

"Not at all," Dr. Dickerson said. The children were glad to see that she was much friendlier than Dr. Snood. "This is my assistant, Tina," she said, motioning to the blond woman beside her. Then she turned back to Pete. "It's here!" she said with a big smile on her face. She looked as excited as the children.

"Are there two mummies?" Benny asked.

"No—one crate holds the mummy, and the other holds its coffin," Dr. Dickerson said. "They're packed very carefully and shipped separately so they won't get damaged. Later, we'll unpack the mummy and put it into its coffin. For now, we've just removed the tops of the crates so we could make sure everything is in one piece." She turned to Pete. "Do you have a stepladder so we can get a look inside?"

Pete went out to a closet in the hall and came back a moment later with a stepladder, which he placed beside one of the crates. Dr. Dickerson climbed up and carefully removed several large pieces of foam rubber that had fit snugly into place over the top of the mummy. At last, she peered down into the crate, and a broad smile spread across her face.

"There he is," Dr. Dickerson said. "Our mummy."

After a moment, she stepped down and Pete climbed up to take a look. "Come on over and see," he said to the Aldens.

Pete stepped down. One at a time, the Aldens climbed up the stepladder and peered into the crate. Inside, they saw what looked like a person lying down, completely covered in cloth bandages. But the person had no face. Where the face should have been, there were just bandages, giving it a strange, creepy look.

"Wow!" said Benny. He couldn't believe there was really a dead body inside. He felt a chill run up his spine.

Henry was the last of the children to look into the crate. He stepped down and Tina stepped up in his place. "Oh, look at that," she said, peering into the crate. But as she shifted her feet on the top of the stepladder, she suddenly fell. "Ow!" she cried out as she landed on the floor.

Everyone rushed over. Dr. Dickerson knelt on the floor beside Tina. "What happened?" she asked, helping Tina to sit up. "Are you hurt?"

Tina grimaced in pain. "My ankle," she said, gritting her teeth. "I think I twisted it."

Dr. Dickerson and Pete looked at Tina's ankle. It was turning pink and beginning to swell. As Pete gently touched her ankle, Tina winced in pain.

"We'd better put ice on that to stop the swelling," Jessie suggested. "I'll run down to the café and get some."

"That would be great," Dr. Dickerson said.

"Yes, thank you," Tina said, her voice filled with pain.

Jessie came back a moment later with the ice. Tina held it on her ankle for several minutes. But her pain did not let up.

"I think we'd better take Tina over to the

hospital," Dr. Dickerson said. "We should get some X rays and see if anything's broken."

Dr. Dickerson drove Tina to the hospital, promising to call as soon as they knew how bad Tina's ankle was.

Pete and the Aldens waited in the prep room. "How would you guys like to see some of the other pieces in the exhibit?" Pete asked, trying to cheer everyone up.

"That would be great," Jessie said, speaking for all of them.

Pete led them over to one of the tables where some things had been unpacked from their boxes and arranged in neat rows. Next to each item was a small card with information printed on it. "These statues show what life was like in ancient Egypt." There was a woman carrying a basket on her head, and a man holding a pitcher. Some of the statues were part human and part animal. "That's how the ancient Egyptians portrayed their gods," Pete explained.

On another table were statues carved

from gray limestone, white alabaster, and yellow jasper. Some were made of clay or wood and were painted in bright colors. There were animal sculptures in gold and silver and bronze. There were also cups and pots, necklaces and bracelets.

"The Egyptians thought that after you died, in the 'afterlife,' you'd need everything you used when you were alive," Pete said. "So they buried their dead with plates, clothes, jewelry, and sometimes even chariots."

"Those two gold cats are beautiful," Violet said.

"I like the funny monkey," said Benny, pointing to a statue of a baboon.

"Over here we have instruments," Pete said, pointing to a wooden flute decorated with gold. "The Egyptians loved to sing, dance, and make music."

"What did children play back then?" Benny asked.

"Well, they didn't have video games or TV," said Pete. "But I think some of their toys will look familiar to you."

"Really?" asked Benny.

Pete pointed to the end of the table.

"Those look like balls," Henry said.

"That's right," said Pete. "Balls, marbles, spinning tops. Imagine — these toys were used thousands of years ago."

"Here's a doll that belonged to a little girl in ancient Egypt," Pete continued. The doll's body was made from a flat board decorated with patterns, and her hair was strung with clay beads. "It looks different from dolls today, but I'm sure the girl who owned it loved it just as much."

Just then the phone rang.

Pete picked up the receiver. "Hello? Yes, Sam. How is she?"

The Aldens watched as Pete's face darkened. "Oh, that's terrible," he said. "I'll see you when you get back."

Pete hung up the phone and turned to the children. "Tina's ankle is broken. She'll have to stay off it for several weeks."

"That's awful!" Violet said.

"Yes, poor Tina," Pete said. "And without

her help, how will we get this exhibit ready in time?"

"She had just looked at the mummy when she fell," said Benny.

Pete frowned. "Maybe it's the mummy's curse," he said.

CHAPTER 2

The Mummy's Curse

"What's the mummy's curse?" Jessie asked.

"Some people believe mummies should not be removed from where they were buried," said Pete. "They believe mummies carry evil spells to punish anyone who disturbs them. *That's* the mummy's curse."

"Really?" Benny asked, his eyes wide.

"A long time ago, when scientists were digging up a mummy, if someone died or got hurt or something else bad happened, people would say it was because of the curse," Pete went on.

"Is there really such a thing?" Violet asked.

"What do you think?" Pete said.

"No. If something bad happened it was just a coincidence," Henry said firmly.

"That's right," Pete said. "There's no such thing as ghosts or magic spells. And there's no such thing as a mummy's curse."

Still, Benny's eyes were wide. "But Tina fell *right after* she looked at the mummy," he said.

"I was just joking before," Pete said kindly. "It was an unfortunate accident, but it wasn't the mummy's fault."

But Benny didn't look as if he believed that. He backed away from the crate holding the mummy. He was afraid he might fall and get hurt, too.

The phone rang again. "Hello?" Pete said, picking up the receiver. "Yes, Reginald, that's right." The Aldens watched as Pete listened to what Dr. Snood was saying. He did not look happy.

"No, it's not a room we normally use," Pete said, "But — "

Again he was silent as Dr. Snood spoke. The children wondered what he was saying.

"All right," Pete said. "I'll see what I can figure out." Then he hung up the phone and sighed heavily.

"Is something wrong?" Violet asked gently.

"Well, if there were a mummy's curse, I'd say it's struck again," Pete said.

"What do you mean?" Benny asked. He sounded nervous.

Pete smiled at Benny's worried look. "Don't worry, Benny. It's not that bad." He patted Benny on the shoulder. "The exhibit was going to be in a hall we don't usually use. That was Dr. Snood on the phone. He said the cleaning crew is too busy to clean the extra room. And there's no money left in the budget to hire an extra crew. Without Tina *and* without the cleaning crew, we'll never get the exhibit ready in time." He sighed again.

"I have an idea," Jessie said.

"You do?" Pete asked, peering wearily over his fingers.

"We could help you," she said.

Pete sat up and smiled. "That's nice, but this is a big job. I'm not really sure you'd be able to help us get our exhibit ready in time."

"But there are lots of things we could do," Jessie said. "We're great cleaners. We could do the work you needed the cleaning crew to do. And we'll do it for free."

"Yeah," said Henry, getting excited. "And we can carry boxes and help Dr. Dickerson. Whatever needs to be done."

Pete was looking thoughtful.

"Why don't you call our grandfather and ask him," Henry suggested.

Pete picked up the telephone, and a few minutes later it was decided. The Aldens had a job. "You start first thing tomorrow," Pete said.

"Great," said Jessie. "We'll be back to-morrow morning, bright and early!"

As they headed out, the children stopped

in the prep room to pick up their jackets, which they'd left there.

While Henry, Jessie, and Violet put on their jackets, Benny turned to look at the two huge crates that were still at the end of the room. He couldn't resist stealing one last peek at the mummy. Benny walked over, got up on the stepladder, and peered down into the crate. The mummy was lying there, just as it had been before. Its blank face pointed up at the ceiling as if it were waiting for something.

Benny thought about the mummy's curse. The room seemed too quiet. He looked up and realized the others had left without him. Suddenly, he felt lonely and a little bit scared. He quickly got down from the stepladder.

"Hey, you guys, wait for me!" he called, running to catch up.

As they were leaving the building, Henry noticed a familiar face in the lobby. It was the woman he'd seen at lunch.

This time, the woman walked right up to

them and introduced herself. "Hi, I'm Lori Paulson. I saw you guys in the café."

"Yes, we were there," Jessie said, surprised to be recognized by a stranger.

"So what have you been doing here all afternoon?" Ms. Paulson asked.

"We got to see the — " Benny began, but Jessie interrupted him.

"What my little brother was starting to say was, we just love this museum. We've been exploring."

"And we got to see the — " Benny began again.

This time, Henry grabbed Benny's arm and pulled him off to the side. "Remember, Pete said the new exhibit is supposed to be a secret," he whispered.

Meanwhile, Jessie was talking to Ms. Paulson. "We're the Aldens. I'm Jessie and this is my sister Violet. Those are my brothers, Henry and Benny."

"It's nice to meet you," Ms. Paulson said.

"What have *you* been doing here all afternoon, Ms. Paulson?" Jessie asked.

"Call me Lori," she said. "I've been . . .

Oh, I just love the museum, too." She smiled, and for a moment Jessie thought she looked uncomfortable. "I come here all the time."

Now Benny remembered not to talk about the mummy. He asked Lori, "Don't you love the dinosaurs?"

"I didn't know they had dinosaurs here," Lori said.

"Not real dinosaurs, of course," Benny said. "But they've got a bunch of skulls and bones in that big room at the back."

"Thanks for telling me," Lori said. "I'll have to check that out."

Jessie looked at her watch. Their housekeeper, Mrs. McGregor, would be putting dinner on the table soon. "I'm sorry, but we've got to be going."

"Oh, um . . ." Lori seemed to want to ask the children something. Finally, she said, "Did I see you talking to the curator at lunch?"

"Yes, Pete Miller is a friend of our grandfather's," Henry said.

Lori's face lit up. "Did he mention anything about the new Egyptian exhibit?"

The Aldens all looked at each other, not sure what to say. They didn't want to lie, but they also knew they weren't supposed to talk about the exhibit.

"He just told us that it was opening in a couple of weeks," Henry said at last.

"What's going to be in the exhibit?" Lori asked. "Will there be a mummy?"

"We've got to go," Jessie said, pointing to her watch. "Sorry."

"But — " Lori began, but the Aldens quickly headed off before she could ask any more questions.

As the Aldens walked down the front steps of the museum, Henry turned to the others. "She was in the cafeteria when we were having lunch. She kept staring at us the whole time."

"I wonder why she's so curious about the new exhibit," Jessie added.

"Maybe she just likes mummies," Benny said. "Like me."

"I get the feeling there's something more to it," Henry said. "You should have seen how she was watching us during lunch. And there's something else strange about her."

"What?" asked Violet.

"She says she comes here all the time. So how come she's never seen the dinosaur bones?" Henry said.

"That is pretty strange," Jessie agreed.

"I think maybe Lori Paulson isn't telling us the truth," Henry said.

"But why would she lie?" Violet asked.

"I bet it has something to do with the Egyptian exhibit she's so curious about," said Jessie.

"Well, I don't know about you guys, but I'm too hungry to worry about Lori Paulson," Benny said. "Let's go home for dinner!"

The next day, the Aldens arrived before the museum opened, ready to work. The building was quiet and almost empty. As they walked down the long, dark hallway to the prep room for the Egyptian exhibit, their footsteps echoed on the hard floor.

A light was shining under the door of the prep room. When the Aldens pushed the door open, they were surprised to see not Sam or Pete, but Dr. Snood. He was standing up on the stepladder, peering down into the mummy's crate. He seemed to be deep in thought.

"Hello, Dr. Snood," Jessie said.

Dr. Snood looked up suddenly. He seemed startled, as if he'd been caught doing something he shouldn't. He quickly stepped down from the stepladder. "I was just . . ." he began, but his voice trailed off.

"The mummy is really cool, isn't it?" Benny asked.

"It isn't *cool*," Dr. Snood snapped. "It is a valuable artifact from four thousand years ago. You must never touch it, or any of the things in this exhibit. Do you understand?"

The Aldens were stunned. Benny was only being friendly. Why was Dr. Snood getting so angry?

"Yes," Henry said. "We understand."

Dr. Snood's eyes moved quickly around the room, as if he were looking for something. Then, picking up his briefcase, he walked out without another word.

CHAPTER 3

Mysterious Footsteps

"I was just trying to be nice," Benny said, looking after Dr. Snood.

"I know," said Violet. "Don't feel bad."

"He's just a grumpy man," said Henry.

"But I wonder why," Jessie said. "Is it just that he doesn't like kids, or is something else bothering him?"

"Did you see how he was looking at the mummy when we came in?" Violet asked.

"And then he seemed so startled when he saw us," Henry added. "As if he'd been doing something wrong."

Before they could say any more, Pete came hurrying into the room. "Hi, kids!" he called out. "Sorry, I got stuck on a phone call. Have you been here long?"

"No," said Henry. "We just got here."

"And ran into Dr. Snood," Benny said.

"He didn't seem to be very happy to see us," Jessie explained. She couldn't help but wonder why Dr. Snood was being so mean to them when they were only trying to help the museum.

"Pete, what's an 'artifact'?" Benny asked, remembering one of the words Dr. Snood had used.

"An artifact is an object made by people a long time ago," Pete answered. "Like all these pieces here — the cups, pots, toys, instruments, and sculptures. We can learn a lot about people who lived a long time ago by studying the things they left behind."

"That makes all these objects very valuable," said Pete. "They're important — and they're also worth lots of money."

"Don't worry, we'll be careful," Benny assured him.

"I know you will," Pete said. "Now how about we get to work? We'll start by cleaning out the exhibit hall next door, where the exhibit will be set up for the public."

The Aldens followed Pete through a side door into a much larger room. It was filled with glass display cases and cardboard boxes. Everything was covered in dust, and the paint on the walls was chipped and peeling.

"Hey, isn't that a model of the solar system?" Henry asked, pointing to a group of balls in different sizes hanging from the ceiling.

"And there are some photographs of the moon over there," Violet added.

"The last exhibit in here was about outer space," Pete explained.

"And now it's just a mess!" Benny said.

"Well," said Jessie, rolling up her sleeves, "where do we start?"

In no time, the Aldens were busy. Pete went through everything in the room, dividing it into things to save and things to throw away.

While they were working, Dr. Dickerson arrived, a big, straw bag over her shoulder and a briefcase in her other hand. "Cleaning up the exhibit hall?" she asked.

"Yes, and the Aldens are helping," Pete said. "Since Tina is out and our cleaning crew can't do the extra work, the kids offered to help get the exhibit ready."

The Aldens waited to hear what Dr. Dickerson would say. They were afraid she might not want their help.

"That's great!" Dr. Dickerson said, a smile slowly spreading across her face.

"We're so glad you like the idea, Dr. Dickerson," said Jessie. "We'll do a great job, I promise."

"You can start by calling me Sam, like my friends do," she said. Then she turned to Pete. "How does Dr. Snood feel about the children helping out? I imagine he wouldn't like the idea." The corners of her

mouth were curled up in a small, mysterious smile.

"He doesn't seem to like kids at all," said Henry.

"You're right about that," said Sam.

"But how would you know that?" Pete asked. "You haven't met Dr. Snood yet, have you?"

"Oh — no, I haven't. But I'm sure I'll meet him soon," Dr. Dickerson said. She looked uncomfortable for a moment. "Anyway, I know how museum directors can be."

"Well, he agreed to it when I told him last night," Pete said. "I think it's because he knows we have no other choice."

As the children were leaving the museum that evening, they heard a voice behind them. "Hey, Aldens!"

They turned around and were surprised to see Lori Paulson walking quickly toward them, her orange bag swinging as she walked. She seemed just as surprised to see them.

"What are you doing back here again?" she asked.

There was an awkward silence as the children wondered what to say. They didn't want to be rude, but they knew the details of the exhibit were a secret.

"We're helping with the new exhibit, but Pete told us not to talk about it," said Henry at last, trying to sound firm.

His answer did not stop Lori from asking, "What's going to be in the exhibit? Did you see a mummy?"

"Actually, we haven't seen anything," Violet said, surprising everyone. She was very shy and didn't usually say much to people she didn't know well. "We've just been cleaning out the exhibit hall upstairs."

"So the exhibit will be upstairs?" Lori said. "And they must be preparing the pieces nearby. . . ." Now she seemed to be talking to herself, almost thinking aloud.

"We've got to get going," Henry said.

"All right!" Lori said. "Thanks!" She seemed to have learned what she wanted to know. She headed off in the opposite direction.

"I hope we didn't just give away something we shouldn't have," said Violet.

The next day, the children returned to the museum. Pete had other work to do, so he had told them to go right upstairs and get to work without him.

The Aldens came down the long, dark hallway. When they reached the exhibit hall, Jessie flipped on a light switch, filling the windowless room with light.

The Aldens carefully packed the last of the old outer space displays into boxes. They were so hard at work that the room remained eerily quiet.

Suddenly, Violet heard some footsteps in the hall. "That must be Sam or Pete," she said, expecting someone to appear in the doorway at any moment. But a few minutes passed, and there was nothing but silence.

"That's funny," said Violet.

"What?" asked Jessie.

"I just heard footsteps in the hallway," Violet said. She went to the door and looked down the long, dark hallway in both directions. There was nobody there.

"Maybe I was imagining it," Violet said.

The children went back to work, and a few minutes later, the sound of footsteps returned. "Hey — do you guys hear that?" Violet asked in a hushed voice.

Everyone listened, but the sounds in the hallway had stopped.

"What was it?" asked Jessie.

"I heard footsteps again," Violet said, going to the door once more. But when she looked out in the hall, there was no one there.

"I heard something, too," said Henry. He looked puzzled.

"What's the big deal?" asked Jessie. "Maybe there was someone in the hall, and whoever it was went into another room."

"But there aren't any other rooms in this part of the museum," Henry said. "Just this exhibit hall and the prep room. Why would someone be up here unless he or she was doing something with the Egypt exhibit?"

"Maybe it was Dr. Snood checking up on us," said Benny.

"Or Lori Paulson," suggested Henry. "She knows the exhibit's up here, and she seems awfully interested in it for some reason."

Suddenly, Benny's eyes grew wide. "Or maybe it was the mummy!"

"Oh, Benny," said Jessie.

"Well, it would sound quiet if it walked," Benny pointed out. "I mean, it's not wearing any shoes." He stood up, closed his eyes, stuck his arms out stiffly, and pretended to walk like the mummy.

The children's laughter was interrupted by Sam's arrival. She walked briskly into the room, carrying a large, straw bag.

"Oh, hello Dr. Dicker — I mean, Sam," Jessie said.

"Did you just get here?" Violet asked. "You weren't in the hallway a few minutes ago, were you?"

"No," said Sam. "Just got here."

"You didn't see anybody out in the hall, did you?" Henry asked.

"Nope," Sam said. "Why?"

"Oh, nothing," Henry said. "We just thought we heard someone a little while ago."

"Really?" Sam looked concerned. "There shouldn't be anybody up here besides us." Then she smiled. "Well, there's nobody there now," Sam said. "I'm glad to see you're getting the room ready. I've got a lot of work to do myself." Sam went into the prep room but came back out a moment later. "Have any of you been in the prep room this morning?" she asked. Her face was grim.

"No, why?" Jessie asked.

"Come see," Sam said.

The children went into the prep room, curious about what was the matter. As soon as they stepped in the door they could see why Sam was upset. The papers on Sam's desk were no longer in neat piles; instead they were moved around, and some had slipped onto the floor. The artifacts, which had been lined up in orderly rows, were now scattered about all over the tables.

The children's jaws dropped open.

"What happened?" asked Violet.

"I don't know," said Sam.

CHAPTER 4

The Mummy's Curse Strikes Again

Sam sighed heavily. "When I left last night, everything was neat and organized."

"You mean, someone came in and messed it up?" said Henry. "Who would do that?"

"And why?" added Benny.

Sam shook her head. "I just don't know."

"Maybe that's what those footsteps were," Violet said. "That might have been someone sneaking in here."

"But you said you didn't see anyone, right?" said Sam.

44

"No, when I looked out no one was there," Violet said.

Sam sighed again. "As if it isn't bad enough what happened to Tina, now this."

"It's the mummy's curse again!" said Benny in a hushed voice.

"Oh, Benny, Pete was just joking about that," Henry said.

"It will take me all day to get everything in order again," said Sam.

"I can help," Jessie suggested.

Sam smiled at her. "That would be great. And from now on, we all have to make sure this door is locked tight when we leave."

Henry, Violet, and Benny went back to the exhibit hall to continue packing up the outer space exhibit. Meanwhile, Sam and Jessie sorted through the papers on Sam's desk and put them back in the correct order. When they'd finished that, they started reorganizing the artifacts.

"These artifacts are very valuable and very fragile," said Sam. "So we must always be very careful when we touch them and always wear protective gloves."

Jessie nodded. She was good at being careful. They slowly began to go through the scattered artifacts. Sam picked up each piece and read off the number written on the bottom. Jessie searched through the printed cards to find the information that went with it.

When Pete arrived at lunchtime, Henry and Violet had just taken the last two boxes to the storage room. "Wow!" he said when he entered. "You've done a terrific job! Now we'll have to do something about those walls."

The Aldens looked around at the scuffed and peeling paint. It did look awful.

"Normally I'd hire a painting crew, but we don't have enough money," said Pete.

"Don't worry. We can handle it," Henry assured him.

"Great. Where's Jessie?" Pete asked.

"In here," Jessie called from the prep room.

Pete and the children joined Sam and Jessie. Sam told Pete about the mess she'd found that morning.

Pete looked as upset as Sam had been. "Who would have been going through your things?" he asked. "Make sure you keep these doors locked. Give Henry a key, too, so the kids can lock up when they go in and out." He headed out the door.

"Ready for lunch, Jessie?" Henry asked. "Pete said we could pick something out in the café."

"All right!" Benny said.

But Jessie wasn't paying attention. She was looking at the tables. She and Sam had gotten all the pieces organized again, but there was still something wrong. She couldn't figure out what it was.

"Jessie?" Henry said again.

"Oh, yes?" she said, startled out of her thoughts.

"Come on, let's go down to the café," Henry said.

As the Aldens left the prep room, Jessie took one last look at the objects on the table. Something just wasn't right.

When the Aldens returned from lunch, Pete called them into the prep room. "We have a surprise for you," he said.

The children walked inside and he motioned to the end of the room where Sam was standing. Where the giant crates had been, there was now a large, wooden box. It was completely covered with elaborate paintings of people and animals.

"What's that?" Benny asked.

"That's the mummy's case — its coffin," Sam explained, leading the children over to look. "We unpacked the crates."

"So that's what was in the other crate," Benny said.

"It's really beautiful," said Jessie.

"The Egyptians painted pictures of their gods on the mummy cases. They'd also paint things that the person liked when they were alive," Sam explained.

"Where's the mummy?" Benny asked.

"You can see for yourself," Sam said. She and Pete carefully lifted the heavy, wooden lid. They laid it on the table beside the coffin.

Everyone peered into the coffin. The mummy was lying inside with a large, painted mask over its face.

"Look at that!" Benny exclaimed.

"That's the death mask. It's molded from the person's face and made to look just like the person," said Sam.

The children stared down at the face in the coffin. Its wide eyes, outlined in black, stared up at them. There was black, straight hair painted on both sides. A gold and red headband painted with fancy designs crossed the brow.

"That's amazing," Jessie said. She couldn't take her eyes off the beautiful mask.

"Do you know how mummies were made?" Sam asked.

"They wrapped up the dead bodies in bandages?" asked Benny.

"That's part of it," Sam said. "Normally when a person dies, the body decays. But the ancient Egyptians came up with a way to preserve the body."

"And then did they wrap it?" Benny asked.

"Yes," said Sam. "They stuffed it with sand or sawdust to keep the body's shape. Then they wrapped it carefully in strips of linen cloth. They put jewels and magical charms in between the layers, to help the dead person reach the afterworld. It took *fifteen* days to bandage a mummy!"

"That's a long time," said Jessie.

Sam continued to explain. "Finally, they put the death mask over the mummy's head and placed the mummy in its coffin."

The children stood for a few more minutes looking into the coffin.

Then Sam said, "I wanted you to see the mummy with its mask on. Now I'm going to put the lid on and keep it closed until the exhibit opens."

Pete helped her lift the heavy, wooden lid off the table and replace it on top of the coffin.

As Jessie followed the others into the exhibit hall, she took one more look around the prep room. She still had the nagging feeling something was wrong. But what?

A few minutes later, the Aldens had begun work on the walls of the exhibit hall. Henry scraped and sanded the areas where the paint was chipped and peeling. Meanwhile, the other three laid drop cloths over the floor of the exhibit hall and the glass cases. When that was done, they began priming and painting. They worked all afternoon.

It was nearly dinnertime when Pete came up to see how they were doing. "It looks much better," he said.

The Aldens finished up the corner they'd been working on and stepped back to look.

"Yes, it does," said Jessie, "if I do say so myself."

She and the others closed up the paint cans and cleaned the brushes and pans before they left. As they were walking out, the Aldens talked about all the interesting things they'd seen and learned about ancient Egypt so far.

"That was cool to learn how they made a mummy," Henry said.

"And I like all those statues," said Violet. "Especially those two gold cats."

"And the baboon," Benny added.

"That's it!" Jessie cried.

"That's what?" asked Benny.

"I noticed something was wrong in the prep room this morning," said Jessie.

"We all did — someone messed everything up," said Henry.

"Besides that," Jessie said. "Even after Sam and I had gotten everything straightened out, I kept thinking something was wrong. But I couldn't figure out what it was. Now I remember — the baboon wasn't with the other statues."

"What do you mean?" Violet said. "Sam said that was everything for the exhibit."

"Well, I didn't see it," said Jessie.

"Maybe Sam just moved it somewhere else," suggested Henry.

"Or maybe whoever messed up the room stole the baboon," Jessie said. "Maybe that's why the room was all out of order — because the person was going through all the statues."

"Was there anything else missing?" Violet asked.

"I don't know," said Jessie. "That was the only thing I noticed."

"Why would someone steal that baboon?" Benny asked.

"Remember, Pete said the objects were all really valuable," Jessie said.

"That doesn't explain why they went through Sam's papers," Henry pointed out. "Those aren't valuable."

"But those papers have information about the artifacts," Jessie said. "Maybe they wanted to read about the artifacts, too." She thought for a moment. "And there's an information card to go with each piece. But I don't remember seeing one for the baboon. If we had, Sam and I would have noticed the statue was missing."

"So the person stole the statue and the card, too?" Violet asked.

"I guess so," said Jessie.

"We'd better tell Sam about this first thing tomorrow morning," said Henry.

"See?" Benny said. "That mummy's curse wasn't just a joke!"

CHAPTER 5

A Thief in the Museum

The Aldens arrived early at the museum the next morning. But this time, the door to the prep room was locked.

"That's good," said Henry. "Now no one can go in and make a mess or steal something."

While the children waited for Sam or Pete to arrive, they finished painting the last wall of the exhibit hall.

They were just cleaning their brushes when Sam appeared in the doorway.

"Hello!" she called, heading into the prep

room. The Aldens quickly put away all the painting supplies and followed Sam.

"Sam, we were wondering . . ." Jessie began. "Are these *all* the pieces for the Egypt exhibit?"

"Yes," Sam said, continuing to unload her bag.

"Are you sure everything's here?" Jessie asked.

Sam looked quickly at Jessie. "What do you mean?"

"Well, the first day we were here, Pete showed us some of the artifacts. And there was a little baboon . . ." Jessie said.

"Yes?" Sam said.

"Where's the baboon now?" Jessie asked.

Sam's eyebrows furrowed. "The baboon? It's . . ." She went over to the tables holding the artifacts and walked slowly from one table to the next. "How odd," she mumbled to herself. She walked around the tables again before walking quickly to the corner where the boxes were stacked. The Aldens watched as Sam picked up one box after another, making sure they were all empty.

At last, Sam turned around and looked back at the Aldens. "I don't know where it is," she said. She looked quickly around the room, but there was nowhere else that the baboon statue could have been.

"So you saw the baboon two days ago?" Sam asked.

"Yes," said Henry. "It was right on the table with the other pieces you'd unpacked."

"I remember because it was my favorite piece," said Benny sadly.

"When did you notice it was missing?" Sam asked.

"Yesterday," Jessie said. "And remember, someone had come in and messed everything up. . . ."

"Oh, my goodness," Sam said, sinking into her chair. "So we have a thief."

Everyone was silent for a moment.

Then Sam spoke. "We mustn't jump to conclusions. The statue may just have been misplaced."

"There may be other things missing, too," Jessie pointed out. "I just happened to notice that piece because it was Benny's favorite. Should I go through the list you have and see what else is missing?"

"No," Sam said. "You kids have done enough work already. Take a break for lunch."

"Shouldn't we tell Pete and Dr. Snood?" Henry asked.

"Yes, definitely," said Sam. "But not until we're really sure it's missing. I don't want to worry them if I don't have to."

When the Aldens came back from the café a short while later, they were pleased to see how bright and clean the exhibit hall looked with its fresh coat of paint.

"Now all we need to do is wash this filthy floor," said Jessie.

"And dust the display cases," Henry added.

Henry and Jessie each took a mop and a bucket from the supply closet and found a bottle of floor soap. Violet and Benny found rags and some glass cleaner.

They were returning to the exhibit hall

when Sam appeared in the doorway. "Jessie, I've decided I could use your help. I've got too many other things to take care of." She handed a set of papers to Jessie. "That's the printout of all the items we're supposed to have in the exhibit. You'll see I made a little *x* next to the baboon. Would you make sure there's nothing else missing?"

"Sure," said Jessie. She followed Sam into the prep room.

Sam sat back down at her desk. Jessie walked slowly around the tables, checking off each item on the list when she'd spotted it. She noted the cups and pots, the doll, the beautiful gold cat statues.

As she flipped through the list, Jessie noted happily that every item had a checkmark next to it except for the baboon, which had an *x*. She was pleased to see that no other items were missing.

Or were they?

Jessie looked back at the table. There had been a wooden flute, hadn't there?

She looked all around the tables, but there was no flute to be seen.

Then she looked at the paper she was holding. Had she somehow missed the listing for the flute? She quickly scanned down the list. The flute was not listed.

"Sam, this is really weird," she said.

"What is it?" Sam asked, looking up from her work. "Is there something missing?"

"No, everything on the list is here," Jessie said.

"Great," Sam said with relief.

"But I remember something that isn't here," Jessie said.

"What?" Sam asked, standing up.

"A wooden flute," Jessie said.

"Yes, of course," Sam said, going to look for herself. "I was planning to put that on display next to the harp. It isn't here?"

"No," Jessie said. "And what's even stranger, it's not on the list, either." She handed the list to Sam.

Sam flipped slowly through the list, looking carefully at each page. "You're right, the flute isn't listed." Then she looked at the tables. "And I don't see it anywhere." Sam made a note at the bottom of the list. "Another missing piece."

"Why isn't it on the list?" Jessie asked.

"I'm not sure," said Sam. "This is the list I got from the Egyptian Museum. Maybe they added the flute later and forgot to put it on the list." Sam smiled at Jessie. "Lucky for me you have such a good memory."

"Are you going to tell Pete about it?" Jessie asked.

"Yes, I'll go right now." Sam walked to the door. Then she turned around and looked back at Jessie. "Don't say anything about this to him, though. I don't think he'd want everyone to know that pieces of the exhibit were missing. You understand, don't you? Bad publicity for the museum."

"Yes, I understand," Jessie said.

After Sam had left, Jessie went into the exhibit hall. She told the others about the missing flute and that it had never even been on the list.

"I can't believe someone has been stealing things from the exhibit," Benny said.

"What's Sam going to do about it?" Henry asked.

"She went to talk to Pete, but she said we shouldn't say anything about it," Jessie said.

"Why not?" Benny asked.

"It would be bad publicity for the museum if people found out," Jessie explained. "Sam figured Pete wouldn't want everyone to know."

"That makes sense," Henry agreed.

"I can't believe there's a list of items that isn't even accurate," said Violet. "What good is that?"

"I have an idea," Jessie said. "Let's make our own list. Then we'll be sure of every- thing that's there — and we'll know if any- thing else disappears."

"Great idea," said Violet. "I'll help you."

"Benny and I will finish cleaning the dis- play cases," said Henry.

Going to her backpack, which she'd left by Sam's desk, Jessie pulled out a small, blue notebook and a pen. She had written her name on the inside cover, but other than that, the notebook was blank. Jessie flipped open to the first page and wrote at the top: *Enter the Mummy's Tomb*. "You look at the table and tell me the items, and I'll write them down," Jessie said.

"Okay," said Violet. "Two gold cat statues . . ." she began. Slowly the girls worked their way around the tables, with Violet telling Jessie what was on each table, and Jessie writing the items in her notebook. She wrote down the name of the object and a short description so she'd remember what it was. It took a long time, but at last, they had an accurate list of everything that was there.

Sam returned as they were finishing the list.

"What did Pete say?" Jessie asked.

"He wasn't in his office," Sam said. "I'll have to catch him later." She looked at Jessie's notebook, which Jessie was just closing up.

"What are you doing?" she asked.

"Since that list wasn't accurate, Violet and I decided to make our own," Jessie said. She handed the notebook over for Sam to see.

"What smart kids you are," Sam said.

Just then they heard a deep voice in the next room. When they looked in, Pete was there talking with Henry and Benny.

"Hi, Pete," Violet said as she and Jessie joined the others.

"I was just telling the boys how great it looks in here." He walked around the room admiring the children's hard work. "Our regular cleaning and painting crews couldn't have done a better job."

The children smiled proudly.

"They've done a fine job, haven't they?" Sam said. "Pete, can I talk to you in here for a moment?"

"Sure," Pete said. "I'll see you tomorrow," he told the Aldens.

The kids knew that Sam was going to talk to Pete about the missing items. They wanted to stay and hear what he planned to do. But it was nearly dinnertime.

"See you tomorrow," Henry called over his shoulder.

CHAPTER 6

An Overheard Conversation

The next day, when the Aldens arrived at the museum, they found Sam carrying a large, framed picture into the exhibit hall.

"What's that?" Benny asked. The painting showed a group of Egyptian men and women. Their bodies were all turned sideways and looked stiff and angular. The edges of the painting under the glass were jagged and uneven.

"It's a painting on papyrus," she said. "That's what the Egyptians used since they didn't have paper. Isn't it amazing how the colors have lasted for thousands of years?"

"How beautiful!" Violet said. She loved to paint and always enjoyed looking at artwork.

"These paintings really make the exhibit complete," said Sam. "You see, the walls of the Egyptian tombs would have been covered with paintings depicting the dead person's life."

"Did you talk to Pete last night about the missing pieces?" Jessie asked.

"Yes," Sam said. "He's going to have new locks put on the doors and make sure the security guard comes by each night. We'll catch the thief." She smiled at Jessie's concerned face. "Don't worry so much."

"I just wish there was something I could do," Jessie began.

"There is," Sam said. "Help me hang these paintings."

The children spent the rest of the morning working with Sam.

First, Sam selected two maps to be mounted on the wall. One was a map of the world, showing the country of Egypt on the continent of Africa.

"Egypt is on the other side of the world from our country," said Violet.

"It's near the equator, so it must be hot there," Henry pointed out.

The other map showed the outline of ancient Egypt. "What's that big, blue line?" Benny asked.

"That's the Nile River," said Sam. "It was very important to the Egyptians. Egypt is a desert with very little rain. The people depended on the Nile for water to live and to grow their crops."

They hung the two maps right by the entrance to the exhibit.

Next, they put up an assortment of paintings that showed Egyptians in many different poses: eating, singing, dancing, and driving chariots.

Other paintings depicted Egyptian gods. They had human bodies and some had the heads of animals.

Some of the paintings had rows of tiny

little pictures. "What are those?" asked Benny.

"Those are hieroglyphics, a kind of Egyptian writing system," Sam said. "It was created over five thousand years ago. The pictures might stand for a sound, a letter, or a whole word."

Sam and the children stood in the center of the hall and looked around slowly.

"I'm going to get Pete to come up and see how great it looks," said Violet.

"I'll come with you," said Benny.

The two went downstairs to Pete's office. His door was closed and it looked dark inside. Violet knocked. As the children waited for an answer, they couldn't help overhearing the conversation in Dr. Snood's office next door, as his door was open.

"I'm worried because Ms. Delaney, the director of the Carson City Museum, called again. They're quite upset over there," Dr. Snood was saying.

"What did she say?" the children heard Pete ask.

"She said the Carson City Museum isn't happy about working with us on next year's festival. They feel we stole the Egypt exhibit away from them," said Dr. Snood.

Violet and Benny looked at each other, their eyes wide.

"That's crazy," Pete was saying.

"Well, that's how they feel," said Dr. Snood. "You know, for the past few years we've always worked well with them. That is, before you started here and suggested this exhibit."

"Maybe there's something we can do," Pete suggested.

"You work on it," said Dr. Snood. His voice sounded angry.

A moment later, Pete emerged from Dr. Snood's office. His face looked serious until he spotted the Aldens. "Violet, Benny," Pete said with a smile. "How's everything going?"

"We've put up all the paintings — want to come see?" Violet asked.

"I'd love to," said Pete. He turned back into Dr. Snood's office. "Reginald, would you like to come see how the Egyptian exhibit is going?"

"I've got to make a phone call," Dr. Snood said. "Then I'll come up for a quick look before my lunch meeting."

When they entered the exhibit hall a few minutes later, Pete broke into a huge grin. "This looks fantastic. I'm sure Dr. Snood will be pleased when he sees it."

Sam, who had been waiting with Jessie and Henry, said, "Oh, is he coming up?"

"Yes, he said he'd come up for a few minutes before his lunch meeting," Pete said.

Sam looked at her watch. "Is it lunchtime already? I've got to run."

"Can't you stay a few minutes to talk to Dr. Snood?" asked Pete.

"No, I'm meeting with the man who's designing the guide for the exhibit, and it may take all afternoon. I'll see you tomorrow." She went quickly into the prep room and grabbed her things. Then she was gone.

Dr. Snood appeared in the doorway a moment later. He walked slowly around the room, looking at the freshly painted walls, the clean glass cases, and the paintings the children had helped put up.

"I must admit, it does look nice in here," he said in a tight voice, as if it were hard for him to say something nice. "And where is Dr. Dickerson?"

"Sam had to leave in a hurry," Pete explained.

"You'd think our expensive Egyptian expert could make time to meet with me. We're certainly paying enough," he said. "Why are all the display cases empty?"

"We just cleaned them yesterday," Jessie said. "Sam is going to arrange the pieces soon."

"So I assume the artifacts are still in the prep room," Dr. Snood said, heading in that direction.

Pete turned to the kids. "I think he's pleased. You've done a great job. Why don't you take the afternoon off, and we'll see you back here tomorrow."

"Okay," Violet said. The Aldens went into the prep room to get their backpacks.

Dr. Snood was there, standing beside one of the tables of artifacts. He was holding one of the gold cat statues, turning it slowly around in his hands. He had a dreamy smile on his face, as if he were thinking of something far away.

As the Aldens watched, he put down the cat and picked up a bright blue sculpture of a hippo. He must have felt the children's eyes on him, because he suddenly looked up. The look on his face changed abruptly. Now he looked as if he'd been caught doing something he shouldn't be. He quickly put the hippo down.

"You kids haven't been touching these, have you?" asked Dr. Snood.

"No, we—" Henry began.

"Make sure you don't," said Dr. Snood in a stern voice. "And make sure the lid on that coffin stays closed."

"Of course—" said Jessie. Before she could say any more, he walked out.

The Aldens stood still for a moment, stunned by Dr. Snood's harsh behavior.

At last Jessie said, "I don't know which

was stranger: the way he was looking at those artifacts or the way he just spoke to us."

"I don't know, either," Henry agreed. "I wonder what he was thinking about when we first came in and he was holding the statues."

"It was as if he were in another world," said Violet.

"And then he got so angry all of a sudden," said Jessie. "And we would never touch the artifacts!"

"Maybe Sam told him about the thief and so he's worried the pieces aren't safe," said Henry.

"He doesn't seem to trust us much," Violet said.

"There was something else, too," Jessie said. "Did you notice how he called Sam 'our expensive Egyptian expert' in that nasty tone?"

"Sounds as if he's upset the museum is paying her so much money," Henry said.

"Or maybe he's jealous," Violet suggested. "Remember, Pete said Dr. Snood used to be a leading expert on Egypt? Maybe he doesn't like the fact that Sam may know more than he does now."

"You guys?" Benny spoke up at last. "Can we go? I want lunch!"

"Sure, Benny," Violet said.

She and Henry picked up their backpacks. But Jessie was still digging around in her backpack when the others were ready to go.

"What's the matter, Jessie?" Violet asked.

"It's nothing. . . . I just can't find . . ." She continued to dig in her backpack. At last she stood up, a puzzled look on her face. "It's not in there."

"What's not in there?" asked Violet.

"My notebook," said Jessie. "The one with the list of artifacts."

"Are you sure you put it in your backpack?" Henry asked.

"I think so," said Jessie.

"Have you looked at it since yesterday?" Violet asked.

"No," Jessie said, still puzzled. It wasn't like her to lose things.

"Maybe you left it around here some-where," Benny suggested.

The children spent the next few minutes searching the prep room — under the ta-bles, on Sam's desk, behind the coffin. Then they moved on to the exhibit hall and looked all over the room. The blue note-book was nowhere to be found.

"Maybe you left it at home," said Violet.

"I don't think so," said Jessie. "I didn't look at it there."

Benny frowned. "The mummy's curse strikes again!"

CHAPTER 7

The Feeling of Being Watched

The next morning, Pete met the Aldens at the door to the prep room. "Sam isn't here yet, but you can wait for her in there."

As Pete headed back down the hall toward the stairs, the children pushed open the door to the prep room. It was dark and quiet inside.

At the end of the room the Aldens could make out the coffin where the mummy lay.

For a moment no one said or did anything. The room felt creepy with no one around but the mummy.

Then Jessie broke the silence. "What are we waiting for? Let's go in." She led the way inside and turned on the light. Suddenly it was just an ordinary room.

"When do you think Sam will get here?" Benny asked.

"I wish she'd told us what she needed us to do today," said Jessie. "We could have gotten started — we have only two days left until the exhibit opens."

"I know what we can work on," Violet said. "Remember Sam said she was meeting with the person who's designing the guide for the exhibit? Well, what if we made a special guide for kids?" Violet asked.

"What do you mean?" asked Jessie.

"It could give some information about ancient Egypt that kids might like to know," Violet said.

"It could explain how they make mummies," Benny put in.

"And we could make up some games and activities about the exhibit, too," Violet added.

"This is like doing a report on Egypt, only more fun," Jessie said. "I'll go down to Pete's office and see if he has some books we can use for research."

"Great idea," Violet said. "I'll come with you."

When they had left, Benny said, "I'll make up some games for the guide. I'm good at games." He looked around the room for a place to sit. It was a small room. Most of it was filled with the tables of artifacts, waiting to be arranged in the display cases. Benny didn't think it would be right to sit down at Sam's desk. The little bit of extra space at the end of the room held the coffin. Benny remembered the mummy's curse and shivered.

"Why don't you go in the exhibit hall? You can sit down on the floor in there," Henry suggested, unlocking the door for his little brother. "I'm going to stay in here and look at the artifacts to get some ideas."

"Okay," Benny said. He pushed open the door to the exhibit hall. There were no windows and it was dark and eerily quiet inside. He felt on the wall for a light switch but didn't feel any. "Henry?" he called back into the prep room.

Henry was concentrating on the artifacts and didn't answer.

"Henry?" he called again.

"Yes?" Henry said at last.

"Where's the light switch?" Benny asked.

"It's over by the main entrance," Henry said.

"Oh, okay," said Benny. All he had to do was walk across the room and turn on the light. But for some reason he felt nervous. He felt as if he weren't alone in the room, as if someone were hiding in the darkness.

"This is silly," he said to himself. "That mummy has me spooked."

Benny began walking across the room. As he walked, he again had a strange feeling that someone was watching him. He could feel someone's eyes on him.

He stopped walking and looked slowly around. "Hello?" he said, his voice shaky in the large, dark, silent room. No one answered. "Hello?" he called again.

Benny felt a prickling sensation on the back of his neck. His palms began to sweat.

He walked quickly to the other door and was relieved when he found the light switch there. He turned it on and looked back around the room. Everything seemed so different in the bright light.

Benny sat down on the floor with his paper and thought for a moment. Then he began to draw a maze. It was supposed to look like a path through a tomb, and you had to find the mummy at the end.

But even with the light on, he didn't feel comfortable. He kept looking over his shoulder, sure that someone, not just a person in a painting, was watching him.

At last, Benny gave up and went back into the prep room to see what Henry was doing. He came in just as Violet and Jessie were returning from Pete's office, their arms full of books.

Henry was standing at one of the tables of artifacts, studying them. He looked upset.

"What's the matter?" Jessie asked.

Henry looked around at all the tables once more before answering.

"Remember that blue hippo that Dr. Snood was looking at?" he asked.

"Yes," Jessie said.

"I don't see it," said Henry.

The other three walked slowly around the tables. After a moment Jessie said, "You're right. It's not here."

"Not again," said Violet, putting down the books she'd been holding on Sam's desk. "That's the third piece missing!"

"Maybe Dr. Snood just put it somewhere else," Jessie said. "He looked very interested in it."

"Yes, maybe that's it," Violet agreed.

"We'll ask Sam when she comes in," Henry said. "We've got to find those pieces before the exhibit opens, and we've got only two days left." Then he noticed the books that Jessie and Violet had brought up. "It looks like you guys found a lot of books."

"We did," said Jessie. "Let's go in the exhibit hall and take a look."

The Aldens went into the next room

and sat down on the floor. They each took a book on their laps and began to flip through them. One book had beautiful photographs of pyramids and maps of Egypt. Another book contained pages of hieroglyphics. And Benny pulled out a book that told how to make a mummy. "Look at this." He pointed to a picture of a shriveled body that had been unwrapped from a mummy. "Gross!"

"But isn't it amazing that you're looking at the face of a person who lived thousands of years ago?" Henry asked.

"I guess so," said Benny, making a face.

Sam arrived a few minutes later. "Why all the grim faces?" she asked.

"Bad news," said Henry. "Another piece is missing. The little blue hippo."

The children all hoped that Sam would say something like, *Oh, that's okay. I just put it in a different room.* But instead, she said nothing. She looked at the children and then walked into the prep room. The Aldens followed as Sam went from table to table, a worried look on her face. Then she sank down into a chair and buried her head in her hands. Henry stood silently beside her, unsure what to do.

"This is terrible," Sam said at last, slowly lifting her head to look at Henry. "When did you notice it was gone?"

"Just this morning," said Henry. "I was looking for it because I remembered that Dr. Snood had been holding it yesterday when we left."

"Dr. Snood was holding it?" Sam said slowly.

"Yes," Henry said.

"That's . . . interesting," Sam said.

"You don't think he would have put it somewhere, do you?" Henry asked.

"I don't know," said Sam. "I hope that's the explanation. I'll have to ask him." She got up slowly and put her briefcase on her desk. "What have you been working on this morning?"

"We're doing a kids' guide for the exhibit," Violet said. The children excitedly told Sam all about it.

"That's a great idea!" Sam said. "I'll

take a look at it when you're done, and we can print copies downstairs." She unloaded some papers from her bag. When she had finished, she said, "I'm going down to speak to Dr. Snood. I'll see you later."

After she'd left, Violet turned to the others. "I hate to think that someone would steal things from the museum."

"I do, too," said Henry. "But what other explanation could there be for the missing pieces?"

"I wonder if it has something to do with the Carson City Museum," Benny said. He told the others what he and Violet had overheard the day before.

"You think someone at the Carson City Museum is so angry at the Greenfield Museum they would try to mess up the exhibit?" Jessie asked.

"Maybe, to make the Greenfield Museum look bad," said Benny.

"I think it's time we paid a visit to the Carson City Museum to see what we can find out," said Henry.

The children stacked the books in a corner of the prep room and gathered up their backpacks. After locking the doors behind them, they headed back home.

When the Aldens got home, they found Grandfather sitting in the living room, reading the paper and drinking a cup of coffee. "You're back early today," he said. "It's not even lunchtime."

"Grandfather, can we go to the Carson City Museum?" Henry asked.

Mr. Alden smiled. "You kids sure have caught the museum bug."

"Well . . ." Jessie looked at her sister and brothers. They hadn't mentioned anything about the missing pieces to their grandfather yet. But they never kept secrets from him. "There have been some strange things going on at the museum," she explained. "First it looked like someone had come into Sam's office and made a big mess. Then a few pieces from the exhibit disappeared."

"Really?" said Grandfather, looking concerned.

"Yes," said Henry. "No one seems to know what's going on."

"But you have an idea?" Mr. Alden asked. He knew the children were excellent mystery solvers.

"We don't know," Henry said. "But we found out that the director of the Carson City Museum was upset they didn't get the Egyptian exhibit. We're wondering if she could have anything to do with the strange things happening at the Greenfield Museum."

"Do you really think she would do something to hurt another museum?" Grandfather looked as if he couldn't really believe it.

"We don't know," said Jessie. "But we thought we'd just take a look around there and see what we can learn."

"You sure are good detectives," Grandfather said. "Whatever you find, I think you'll enjoy that museum. It has some nice exhibits."

Mr. Alden went to a cabinet in the front hall and pulled out a map. "Here are the bus routes to Carson City," he said as he unfolded the map and laid it on the dining room table. The children gathered around to look.

"You'll take the number-seven bus," Grandfather said, pointing to a purple line. "You see, it starts here in Greenfield and goes to Carson City. The bus will let you off at the museum." He traced the bus route with his finger.

"Sounds easy enough," said Henry.

Grandfather folded up the map and handed it to Jessie. He gave each of the children two tokens for the bus. "One for the way there, and one for the way home." The children tucked the tokens into their pockets. "You can get the bus right down at the corner. Call if you need me."

"All right," Jessie said as the children headed out the door. "We'll be home by dinnertime."

The children walked down to the corner, where a street sign and a bench marked the bus stop.

"Remember to stick together," Henry

said. "We don't want anyone to get lost."

The others nodded.

A few minutes later, a large, white bus pulled up to the stop. The children boarded the bus and put their tokens in the box. Then they found seats near the back of the bus.

The bus ride took about fifteen minutes. They were going down a busy street when Henry said, "I see the museum up ahead." He pulled a cord to signal the bus driver, and the bus came slowly to a stop at the next corner.

"Come on, you guys," Henry said, leading the way off the bus.

The children stood for a moment looking up at the museum before they went in. It was much larger than the Greenfield Museum, with white marble steps and columns in the front. There were three colorful banners hanging down between the columns, describing the exhibits on display. THINGS THAT SLITHER, read one banner with a large picture of a snake. Another banner said, CELEBRATIONS AROUND THE WORLD, and had a picture of a globe. The last said, GREAT PAINTERS OF OUR CENTURY.

"Well, here we are," said Jessie. "Let's go in and see what we can find out."

The children entered the lobby and paid the fee to enter. "Where should we go first?" Violet asked. They all looked around the lobby, which was much larger and more crowded than the one at the Greenfield Museum. None of them was really sure what they were looking for, or where they should look.

"I want to see that snake exhibit!" said Benny.

"Sounds like as good a place to start as any," said Henry.

The children went into the snake exhibit and walked around looking at interesting pictures of snakes and other reptiles. There were skeletons of giant boa constrictors and crocodiles, and diagrams of how their bodies work. Benny's favorites were the cases containing live snakes and lizards. A man who worked at the museum took out some iguanas and snakes for the children to touch and hold.

"That was great!" Benny said as the children headed into the exhibit next door, which was about holidays in different countries.

After that, the Aldens took a break for ice cream in the museum's café. It was similar to the one at the Greenfield Museum, but bigger.

"So far we haven't learned anything," said Jessie, disappointed.

"That's not true," said Benny. "We've learned a lot about snakes!"

"And how they celebrate New Year's in China," Violet added.

"That's true," said Jessie. "But we haven't learned anything to help us solve the mystery at the Greenfield Museum."

"That may be about to change," Henry said.

"What do you mean?" Violet asked, turning to look in the direction he was staring. Then she said, "I don't believe it!"

Jessie and Benny looked over to see Lori Paulson entering the cafeteria.

CHAPTER 8

A Museum Spy

As the children watched, Lori Paulson walked slowly down the cafeteria line. As usual, she had her bright orange bag slung over her shoulder. She selected a large cookie wrapped in plastic wrap and a cup of coffee. After she'd paid, she walked over to a table near the window. But as she went to sit down, her bag slipped off her shoulder and fell to the floor. A large pile of papers spilled out. Some slid beneath the table. "Oh, no!" she cried. "I'm so clumsy! I can't believe I just dropped all my stuff."

"I do that, too, sometimes," Violet said kindly, picking up some of the papers.

"I've had a really long day," Lori said.

"Really? Doing what?" Violet asked.

"Oh, I've just been here . . ." Lori said, and her voice trailed off.

"You've been here all day?" Violet asked. "You must really like going to museums."

"I do," Lori said. She smiled at Violet and then picked up the rest of her papers.

"What exhibits did you look at?" Violet asked.

"Oh, er . . . the dinosaurs," Lori said.

"Is there a dinosaur exhibit here, too?" asked Violet.

"Oh—no," Lori said. "I must have been thinking of the Greenfield Museum."

Violet said, "That dinosaur exhibit is great, isn't it?"

Then Lori sighed. "You know, actually I didn't see it. I only went to the Greenfield Museum because, well, there was something I was looking for. Something I had to get."

Violet was confused. "Oh," she said.

She wondered what Lori was talking about. Why did her story keep changing?

Violet reached under the table to get the last piece of paper. As she pulled it up, she saw it was a letter addressed to Lori with the words CARSON CITY MUSEUM at the top.

Lori glanced down at the letter Violet was holding. "Thank you for your help." She took the letter quickly, as if she was afraid Violet might try to read it. She stuffed it into her bag.

Just then a woman in a dark blue suit came into the cafeteria. "Ms. Paulson?" she said as she came over. "I'll be upstairs in my office in a minute if you want to talk."

"All right, Ms. Delaney. I'll be there," said Lori.

"Thanks for the help!" Lori said to Violet as she picked up her coffee and her cookie. "I've got to run."

Violet walked back to where her sister and brothers were.

"What was she doing here?" Henry asked, and then ate some of his ice cream.

"I don't know," said Violet, picking up

her spoon. "She seemed really nervous. She said she liked the dinosaur exhibit."

"Do they have one here, too?" Benny asked hopefully.

"That's what I asked," said Violet. "And she said she must have been thinking of the Greenfield Museum. But when I asked her how she liked that exhibit, she admitted she was really just at the Greenfield Museum because she was looking for something. Something she had to get," Violet said.

"I wonder what she meant by that," said Henry.

"Do you think she meant she had to get a sculpture of a baboon? Or a blue hippo? Or a flute?" Benny asked.

"Why would she steal those pieces?" Jessie asked.

"Maybe for the same reason most thieves steal things — for the money," said Henry. "Pete said they were very valuable. Or maybe she's a collector and she likes Egyptian art."

"Listen, you guys," said Violet. "It gets weirder. One of the things that fell out of her bag was a letter from the Carson City Museum."

"Why would someone here be writing to her?" Henry asked.

"I don't know," Violet said. "All I saw was that it was addressed to her. I wasn't going to read it. But before I could even give it back to her, she grabbed it, as if she didn't want me to see it."

"How odd," said Jessie.

"And then that woman came in and said that Lori should come upstairs to her office to talk," said Violet.

"Who was she?" asked Henry.

"I don't know," said Violet. "Her name was Ms. Delaney."

"We know she works for the museum if she has an office upstairs," Jessie pointed out.

"That name sounds familiar," said Benny.

"Let's go ask at the front desk," suggested Henry.

The children finished their ice cream and threw their garbage in the trash can. Then they headed out to the front desk.

"Excuse me?" Henry asked the man sitting there. "Is there a Ms. Delaney working here?"

"Ms. Delaney?" the man repeated. "Yes. She's the director of the museum."

"The director?" Henry said. "Oh, thank you."

As the Aldens walked away, Benny turned to the others, an excited look on his face. "That's why that name is familiar! She's the one Dr. Snood said had called him because she was angry about the Egypt exhibit!"

"Why do you think Lori is talking to her?" Jessie wondered.

"Do you think Lori's working for the Carson City Museum?" Henry asked.

"Doing what?" asked Violet.

"I'm not sure. Maybe trying to get information about the Egypt exhibit," Henry suggested.

Benny's eyes opened wide. "Like a spy?"

"Or maybe even more than that," Jessie said. "Maybe Ms. Delaney is so angry at the Greenfield Museum that she's hired Lori to ruin the exhibit."

"So you think Lori stole those pieces for

the Carson City Museum?" Violet asked.

"It could be," said Jessie.

Sam was working in the prep room when the Aldens arrived the next morning. When they asked her about the missing pieces, she said only that she didn't want to talk about them.

"She seems upset," Violet whispered to Jessie. The children spent the morning helping Sam arrange the artifacts in the glass cases. Only Henry and Jessie were allowed to carry the pieces. Benny and Violet brought the description cards to place beside them. Sam carried the most delicate pieces herself.

The children also worked on their guide. They studied the books Pete had lent them. Sam let them use her computer and printer. Jessie wrote an introduction to the exhibit. Henry typed up a brief description of ancient Egypt. Violet, who was an excellent artist, traced a map. She also copied some hieroglyphs out of a book and made a chart showing what each word meant. And she drew a beautiful picture of a mummy's death mask for the cover. Benny finished his maze and added a comic strip about mummy making.

When all the pieces of the guide were complete, they gave them to Sam. "Would you take a look at these, please?" Henry asked. "We want to make sure we didn't make any mistakes."

"I'd be happy to," Sam said, sitting down at her desk to read the children's work.

As Jessie stood next to Sam, she noticed a framed photograph on her desk. It showed four small cats lying on a bed. "Are those all your cats?" Jessie asked.

"Yes, those are my beauties," Sam said. "I have a weakness for cats."

A few minutes later, Sam had read through everything. "This looks great! You can make copies on the machine outside Pete's office," she suggested as she headed out to get some lunch. "Don't forget to lock the door when you go."

The children took all the pages and locked the door to the prep room behind them. As Sam had told them, they went downstairs to the copy machine by Pete's office. They made a stack of copies and stapled the pages together into little booklets. On top of each stack they put a copy of Violet's death mask cover.

The children were quite pleased with their work. They each picked up a pile of guides and headed toward the stairs.

But they stopped abruptly when they saw who was sitting a little way down the hall, outside Dr. Snood's office.

It was Lori Paulson.

"Not again!" Henry said.

Lori didn't notice them because she was studying a small, blue notebook she held in her lap.

"Hey!" Jessie cried. "That's my notebook!"

Lori looked up then. She stood up and started walking toward the Aldens. "Is this yours?" she asked, holding the notebook out in front of her.

"Yes," said Jessie. "It is."

"I saw your name on the inside cover," Lori said. "How convenient that you guys happened to be right here."

"Yes, how convenient," said Jessie suspiciously as Lori placed the notebook on top of the pile of guides she was holding. "Where did you find it?"

"It was right there on that bench," Lori said.

Jessie nodded slowly. She didn't remember carrying the notebook down here. How had it ended up there?

Benny groaned. His arms were getting tired from holding the stack of guides. "Can we get going before I drop these?"

"Sure," Jessie said. "See you later, Lori."

The Aldens walked back up to the exhibit hall and put the guides down on one of the glass cases. Sam was still gone.

"How did your notebook end up down on that bench?" Violet asked.

"That's just what I was wondering," said Jessie. "I don't remember bringing it down there."

"Maybe Lori didn't really find it there," Henry said.

"What do you mean?" Benny asked.

"Maybe she took the notebook," said Henry.

"I don't understand," said Benny. "Why would she take it?"

"She wanted to know all about the exhibit, right?" said Henry. "What better way to find out than by looking in Jessie's notebook, which listed everything?"

While he was talking, Jessie was slowly turning the pages of her notebook. The look on her face was growing more and more concerned.

"What is it, Jessie?" Violet asked.

"I think somebody's changed what I wrote!" said Jessie. She laid the book down on the display case where they could all see. She pointed to one of the items on the list. It had been crossed off so heavily it was hard to see what was written beneath. "See here? I don't remember crossing anything off." She flipped to another page. "And here, where it says 'gold cat statue'? I had written '*two* gold cat statues.' Someone crossed out the *two* and the *s* at the end."

"But why?" Henry wondered.

"I have a feeling I know," Jessie said. But before she explained, she started walking around the room, looking at the display cases. At last, she stopped in front of one of the cases. "There's one of the gold cat statues," she said. "But where's the other one?"

The children looked all around, but the other cat wasn't there.

"So you think Lori changed what was in here so you wouldn't remember there had been two cats?" Violet asked.

"Yes," said Jessie.

"Or maybe it wasn't Lori," said Henry. "Remember, Dr. Snood was holding that gold cat and he had that strange smile on his face? Maybe Lori wasn't lying about finding the notebook. Maybe it really was outside Dr. Snood's office. Maybe *he's* the one who stole the pieces and changed what was written in here."

"Why would he steal things from his own museum?" Benny asked.

"I don't know," said Henry. "But he's always acting so strange—holding the pieces as if they belonged to him, and yelling at us to make sure we don't touch them."

"He does collect Egyptian artifacts. Remember, they're all over his office," Jessie said. "Maybe he has even more at home — ones he's stolen."

"Or maybe he's the one trying to ruin the exhibit!" Henry said all of a sudden. "He's been against this exhibit from the start. Maybe he wants to prove he's right by making sure the exhibit fails."

"You know there's one person we haven't talked about," said Violet.

"Who's that?" Jessie asked.

"Sam," Violet said. "It would be really easy for her to steal these things."

"But why would she want to ruin her own exhibit?" asked Henry. "That would only make her look bad."

"That's true," said Violet.

A few minutes later, Pete came upstairs. "The exhibit looks great," he said, strolling from one display case to the next. "I can't believe we got it ready in time for tomorrow's opening!" He grinned at the Aldens. "Thanks to you guys."

"We enjoyed helping," Jessie said.

"Yes. We're having a little party tomorrow night," Pete explained. "We've invited the museum members and also the press. And of course you all must come."

"We'll be there!" Henry said.

"I have one more job for you to do," Pete said. "Would you call the local newspapers and remind them to come to the opening?"

"Why do you invite them?" Benny asked.

"They'll write articles about the exhibit in their newspapers," Pete explained. "When people read them, they'll want to come see for themselves. That's how we'll make sure we get lots of visitors for the exhibit."

"We'd be happy to call," said Henry.

"Great," Pete said. "The list of names and numbers is in my office. You can sit there and use my phone while I get some lunch."

"Okay," said Benny. "As long as you bring some back for us!"

CHAPTER 9

A Scary Surprise

The Aldens used Pete's office to make their phone calls.

Henry had already spoken to a man at the local television news station. Now he was calling the local radio station. "Hello, I'm calling from the Greenfield Museum," Henry said, just as Pete had told him to. "I wanted to remind you about the opening tomorrow night of our latest exhibit, 'Enter the Mummy's Tomb.'"

"We'll have someone there to cover it," said the man on the other end.

"Great," said Henry, hanging up the phone. Jessie checked the radio station off her list.

"Next is the *Greenfield Daily News,* the local paper," said Jessie. "The number is 555-6444."

Henry dialed and listened to the phone ring a few times. Then a woman answered.

"Hello, *Greenfield Daily News,*" she said. "Can I help you?"

"Hello," Henry said. "I'm calling from the Greenfield Museum to remind you of our opening tomorrow night."

" 'Enter the Mummy's Tomb,' " said the woman. "Don't worry, we'll definitely send a reporter and a photographer."

"Yes, thank you," he said, sounding puzzled. He hung up the phone.

"What's the matter, Henry?" Benny asked.

"That was strange," he said.

"Why? What did they say at the newspaper office?" Violet asked.

"It wasn't what the woman said," Henry said slowly. "It was her voice. It sounded so familiar."

"Maybe it was some friend of Grandfather's," Benny suggested.

"Maybe," said Henry, puzzled.

"Anyway, we have a few more names to call," Jessie reminded him.

The children were finishing the phone calls when Dr. Snood came in.

"Where's Pete?" he asked.

"He's getting lunch," Jessie said. "He asked us to make some phone calls about the opening."

Dr. Snood turned and started to leave. He called over his shoulder, "Does Dr. Dickerson have everything ready?"

"Yes, she does," Henry said.

Dr. Snood stopped abruptly and turned around. He looked at Henry strangely. "*She?*" he repeated. "Sam Dickerson is a woman?"

"Haven't you met her?" Jessie asked.

Dr. Snood shook his head. "I've been so busy the past two weeks. Whenever I've gone up there, Dr. Dickerson hasn't been in. Pete scheduled a meeting for the three of us and . . ." He paused and then said awkwardly, "*she* couldn't come. Anyway, it doesn't matter. I saw the exhibit and it looks excellent." He walked slowly out of Pete's office.

"That's weird he never even met her," said Violet.

"Well, Sam did keep some pretty strange hours," Jessie pointed out as she placed the list on Pete's desk. "She'd come in late, leave all of a sudden, you know."

The Aldens left the office and went back upstairs. As they entered the prep room, Sam was there, talking on the phone. "Oh, you'll love this little cat," she was saying to the person on the other end. When she saw the children, she quickly stopped talking. "I'll speak to you later."

She hung up the phone.

"I was telling my friend about the new kitten I just got," Sam explained.

"*Another* one?" Jessie said.

"I couldn't resist," said Sam. She picked up her bag and put it over her shoulder. "Everything's ready for tomorrow. I'm heading home now."

"Hey, wait a minute," Benny said, noticing the coffin at the back of the room. "What about the mummy? Isn't that going to be part of the exhibit?"

"Of course," Sam said. "We'll move the coffin in tomorrow and open the lid. See you tomorrow at seven. Lock up when you go." She headed off down the hall.

The Aldens picked up their backpacks. "Well, tomorrow's the day," Jessie said, "and the exhibit's all ready."

"Looks like we beat the mummy's curse!" Henry said, giving Benny a playful punch on the shoulder.

Before he left, Benny took one last look around the prep room. At the back of the room was the brightly painted coffin. Benny walked over and gently placed his fingers on the edge of the lid, which was shut tight.

"Good night, mummy," Benny whispered. "Tomorrow's your big day."

The next day, the Aldens were at home eating lunch when Benny said, "I can't wait until tonight to see the opening of the exhibit."

"I just hope nothing else goes wrong," said Violet.

"Maybe we could just stop in and see if they need any last-minute help," Jessie said.

The Aldens biked over to the museum. When they arrived, they found Pete and Dr. Snood in the lobby. Pete was standing beside a pair of signs that read:

Enter the Mummy's Tomb
Upstairs Exhibit Hall
Opening at 7:00 This Evening
By Invitation Only

The signs were mounted on sturdy metal stands. With them was a pair of metal poles linked by a red velvet rope.

"Hello!" Pete said when he saw the children. Dr. Snood said nothing.

"Any last-minute jobs you need done?" Henry asked.

"None that I can think of," said Pete. He looked at Dr. Snood, who shook his head. "Sam isn't coming in until later, and we haven't even gone upstairs yet." Pete placed one of the signs in the center of the lobby, next to the main desk. He stood back to see how it looked.

Then he turned to the Aldens. "Actually, there is something. Can you put these up in front of the entrance upstairs so no one will go in until tonight?" He motioned to the sign and velvet rope.

"We'd be happy to," Henry said, picking up the sign.

Jessie and Violet each took one of the metal poles. They walked slowly upstairs.

As they came down the hall, they could see that both the prep room and the exhibit hall were dark and deserted.

But when they reached the prep room, they stopped short.

Something was wrong.

The door of the prep room was open. The children had locked the door before they'd left the night before. Who would have opened it? Pete had said Sam wasn't in yet, and he and Dr. Snood hadn't been upstairs that morning. The only other person who would have a key was the security guard, and she had no reason to go in there.

Had someone broken into the prep room?

The children looked at each other silently. "What's going on?" Henry said quietly.

Jessie shrugged her shoulders.

"Hello?" Henry called, slowly pushing the door open farther. The door creaked as it slowly swung open.

The Aldens peered into the dark room. Everything looked just as they had left it the evening before. Sam's papers were stacked neatly on her desk. Her chair was pushed in underneath. The coffin was still at the back of the room.

Jessie bent down and studied the lock on the door.

At last Violet asked what they were all wondering. "Did someone break in?"

"Looks that way," Henry said. "We locked the door last night, so whoever it was must have picked the lock."

"Wait a minute," Jessie said suddenly. "If someone was trying to get in, they'd pick

the lock from the *outside*, right?" she asked.

"They'd have to," said Henry.

"Well, look at these scratch marks." The children bent and looked where Jessie was pointing.

"So?" Benny asked.

"If someone was trying to get in, he or she would be on the outside of the door, right?" Jessie asked. "But the scratches are on the *inside*."

"So this lock was picked from the inside," Henry said.

"So that means . . ." Violet began.

"Someone was trying to break *out*," said Jessie.

The children looked back into the room. They looked all the way down to the other end where the coffin lay. And then they noticed something they hadn't noticed before.

Something even more frightening than the picked lock.

The lid of the coffin was open.

CHAPTER 10

The Truth Comes Out

"It was the mummy!" Benny cried. "It escaped!"

The lid of the coffin wasn't completely open, but it was pushed back several inches. It definitely was not the way it had been left the night before.

From across the room, it was too dark to see if the mummy was still inside.

"That's ridiculous, Benny," said Jessie. But she didn't sound sure.

"Then who was it?" asked Benny.

"I don't know," said Jessie. "But it wasn't

the mummy. The mummy has been dead for thousands of years."

"Come on, let's go take a closer look," Henry said.

The children began walking slowly to the other end of the dark room. They didn't take their eyes off the coffin. Benny lagged behind, afraid of what they might find — or not find — when they got there.

The coffin was exactly where it had always been, its painted designs visible even in the dim light. When they'd crossed the room, the children stood a few feet away, just looking at it.

They knew the mummy couldn't get up and move. They knew, as Jessie said, that it had been dead for thousands of years. But in the darkness, with the lid of the coffin slightly open, somehow anything seemed possible.

Henry took a few steps closer.

He was trying to peer inside the gap left where the lid had been pushed back. But the light was so dim that it was hard to see.

"Is the mummy still there?" Benny asked nervously.

"Yes, I think so," Henry said, squinting and moving closer.

"This is silly," Jessie said at last. She walked quickly back to the door and switched on the light.

Henry stepped up to the coffin and looked in. He could see the magnificent death mask peering up at him from inside the coffin. "Yes, there it is," he said, breaking into a smile.

The others breathed a sigh of relief and moved closer to see for themselves.

"There's something else in there, too!" Benny cried, pointing in the coffin.

The other children peered in. There was a large, straw bag tucked in next to the mummy.

"That's Sam's bag," Violet said. "What's it doing in there?"

Benny looked inside. All he saw inside was a brown-paper bundle. He put it up on the table. Before Henry could stop him, Benny had begun unwrapping it.

"I don't think you should —" Henry began. But he stopped speaking when he saw what was in the package. "I don't believe it!" he said.

"It's the missing gold cat," Benny said.

The children looked at each other, speechless.

"I'll go get Pete," Jessie said, walking toward the door.

A few moments later, Jessie returned with Pete — and Dr. Snood.

Jessie showed them the lock on the door. "See, here are the scratches."

The two men studied it. "This was definitely picked from the inside," Dr. Snood agreed. "Just as you said."

Then they walked to the back of the room and looked at the open coffin. "You children didn't open this?" Dr. Snood asked.

The children all shook their heads.

"Help me," Dr. Snood said to Pete. Together they lifted the lid off and placed it gently on the table. Then they both walked slowly around the coffin, examining the mummy and the death mask.

"I don't know why someone opened the coffin, but fortunately the mummy doesn't appear to be damaged," Dr. Snood said at last. He sounded relieved.

"There's something else," Henry said.

Dr. Snood looked up from the mummy. "What is it?"

Henry motioned to the gold cat. "We just found this — in Sam's bag," said Henry.

Dr. Snood picked up the statue. "In her bag, you say?" He strode over to Sam's desk. "I don't know what's going on, but I think it's time I had a word with Dr. Dickerson." He picked up the telephone.

"No," Jessie said.

Dr. Snood spun around in surprise.

"I mean, please let me call," said Jessie quickly. "I have a plan."

Dr. Snood looked at her for a moment and then nodded. "All right," he said.

Jessie picked up the phone and dialed number. She looked nervous. "Hello, she said after a moment. "It's Jessie, museum. Pete asked me to give you He needs to see you."

She listened for a moment before she spoke again. "I don't know, he didn't say. He just asked that you come right away."

Again she listened, then said, "No, Dr. Snood is out at a meeting."

At last Jessie smiled. "All right, we'll see you soon."

She hung up the phone.

"Why did you tell her that — about Pete asking you to call and Dr. Snood being out?" Henry asked.

"I know it isn't right to lie," Jessie said. "But I didn't think Sam would come if she knew *Dr. Snood* wanted to see her. I've noticed that she's always avoiding him."

"That does seem to be true," Dr. Snood agreed.

"I guess you might say I've . . . set a trap," Jessie said.

"Very smart, young lady," Dr. Snood admitted.

Jessie smiled and felt her cheeks turning pink.

Pete grinned. "I told you these kids were good."

"I have a question," said Henry. "Has Sam told either of you about the pieces missing from the exhibit?"

"What?" the two men said. They looked at each other and then back at the children.

"Pieces *missing*?" asked Pete. "I've heard nothing of the kind."

"Neither have I," said Dr. Snood.

"We noticed some pieces missing, like a small baboon sculpture, and the little blue hippo, and a flute, and this gold cat. Sam said she had told you," said Jessie.

"No one said anything to me," Dr. Snood said. He seemed to be straining to remain calm. "When Dr. Dickerson comes, we'll get to the bottom of this. Pete and I will wait in here until she comes," Dr. Snood said, stepping into the exhibit hall.

When the two men had gone, Violet said sadly, "I hate to think that she's the one who's been stealing the pieces all along. She's so nice."

"I agree," said Jessie. "But she could still be a thief."

The Aldens waited for Sam to come. No

one felt much like talking. The only sound was the clock ticking on the wall.

Finally, the children heard footsteps in the hallway. "That must be her now," Jessie whispered.

The footsteps came closer, and then Sam stood in the doorway. "What's the matter?" she asked.

Then she spotted the statue on the table. "What's this doing in here? I put this —" She stopped abruptly as Dr. Snood stepped into the room, with Pete behind him.

For a moment, Sam and Dr. Snood just looked at each other.

Then a slow smile spread across Dr. Snood's face. It was not a happy smile. Instead, he looked very, very angry.

Sam sighed heavily and looked at the ground.

"So it's you," Dr. Snood said, his voice tight. "Even under all that red hair, I'd recognize you anywhere. I hoped I'd never see you again."

"Hello, Reggie," Sam said.

"What's going on?" asked Benny.

Dr. Snood turned to the children. "We've found our thief," he said. "Her name is Samantha Peters."

"It was," said Sam. "I've married. Now I'm Samantha Dickerson."

"You two know each other?" Pete asked.

"Yes," said Dr. Snood. "Dr. Peters — or Dr. Dickerson, if you prefer — was my partner many years ago, before I became the director here. We were digging in an Egyptian tomb. She was a brilliant Egyptologist, and everything was going well. Until I realized I could never work with her again."

"Why?" asked Benny.

"Shall I tell them?" Dr. Snood asked Sam.

She looked away, refusing to answer.

Dr. Snood turned back to the children. "She suggested we might take a few 'souvenirs' from the dig — small statues to keep for ourselves or sell. I told her, definitely not. But it sounds as if that's exactly what she's been doing here."

"Is it?" Violet asked Sam in a soft voice.

Sam was looking at the floor. She sighed again. At last she looked up at the faces of the children. Her face looked sad and tired. "Yes, I have," she admitted at last. "When Pete asked me to run this exhibit, I was very happy. I haven't been making much money lately. I thought I'd be able to pocket a few pieces and make some quick cash. I was planning to sell them to a rich collector I know."

"That's who you were talking to on the phone about a cat, wasn't it?" asked Jessie.

"Yes," Sam said. "When I found out that Dr. Snood was the director here, I was afraid he'd catch me. So I had my hair curled and dyed red. I went by my married name and called myself Sam so people would assume I was a man. Unless they met me, of course."

"So that's why you've been avoiding Dr. Snood," Jessie said.

"Yes," said Sam. "When Tina got hurt, I was pleased that Pete suggested you children would help me. I figured I could slip anything past a bunch of kids." She raised her eyebrows. "But I didn't realize who I was dealing with. You Aldens are smart. And you don't give up."

"No," Henry said. "We don't. Not until we've solved the mystery."

"So you never told anyone that those pieces were missing, did you?" asked Violet.

"Of course not," said Sam. "I didn't think you'd even notice if a piece was gone here and there. That's why I didn't take them all at once. I hadn't counted on you having such good memories. I had to pretend I was surprised each time you noticed another one missing. But I figured that if you kids were the only ones who knew, then I was safe."

"But then why did you give me that list to make sure nothing was missing?" asked Jessie.

"I made up that list myself. I left off the pieces I'd already taken," Sam said.

"What about my notebook?" Jessie asked. "Did you take it?"

"I did," Sam said. "You let me look at it,

and I never gave it back. I changed it, too. I tried to make it look like your handwriting, so you wouldn't realize. Then I left it by Dr. Snood's office, so you'd think he'd taken it, not me."

"What about the lock on the door and the open coffin?" asked Henry. "Did you do that?"

Sam nodded. "That's where I was hiding the pieces," she said.

"In the coffin?" Benny asked, shocked.

"I knew no one would look in there," she said. "Last night I came back here very late, after everyone had left. I was planning to take out the last of the pieces. But then the security guard came by, just as I was about to leave. I quickly turned off the lights so she wouldn't see me. But then she did something I hadn't expected." Sam laughed a short laugh. "She thought no one was in here, so she locked the door. I was locked in."

"And you had to break out," Henry said.

"Exactly," said Sam. "Good thing I know how to pick a lock. But in my hurry I left the coffin open and forgot to lock the door behind me. And I accidentally left the most valuable piece here — that gold cat."

While they were talking, Pete had quietly gone over to the telephone and made a phone call. A police officer appeared in the doorway just as Sam was finishing her story.

As the police officer led her away, Pete said, "It looks as if the mummy's curse is on Sam."

James Alden and his grandchildren arrived at the museum that night just before seven o'clock.

"I can't wait to see how everyone likes the exhibit," Benny said.

"And I can't wait to see what you've all been working on," Grandfather said.

"Hello, Aldens," Pete said, coming over as soon as he saw them. He brought Dr. Snood with him. The Aldens were surprised to see how happy Dr. Snood looked.

"James, good to see you," Pete said. He introduced Dr. Snood to James Alden.

"The exhibit looks great," said Grandfather.

"We couldn't have done it without your grandchildren," Pete said.

"I must admit I had my doubts at first," Dr. Snood said. "But I was wrong. They did a great job with the exhibit — and they caught a criminal!"

"That is their specialty," Grandfather said proudly.

"Can I tell you something, Dr. Snood?" Jessie asked in a quiet voice.

"Yes," Dr. Snood said.

"We thought *you* might be the thief," she said.

"*Me?*" he said. And then he did something they had never seen him do. He began to laugh. "Why me?"

"Well, we kept seeing you looking at the pieces, and then they'd be missing," said Jessie. "And there always seemed to be something bothering you."

Dr. Snood was silent for a moment. Then he spoke. "You children are wise beyond your years. There has been something bothering me, and it took this exhibit for me to realize it."

"Realize what?" Pete asked.

"I realized, as I watched this exhibit being put together, how much I miss Egyptology. That's my real love. So I'm stepping down as director. I'm going to lead a dig in Egypt next year."

"Excuse me," said a voice behind the children.

They turned around and were surprised to see Lori Paulson.

"Hello, Ms. Paulson," Pete said.

"What are you doing here?" Benny couldn't help asking.

Suddenly Henry laughed. "I think I know," he said. "You're a reporter for the *Greenfield Daily News*, aren't you?"

"How did you know?" Lori asked, surprised.

"When I called the newspaper yesterday, you were the one who answered, weren't you?" Henry said.

Lori nodded.

"I knew your voice was familiar," Henry

explained. "I just didn't figure out it was you until now."

"I've just started working there," Lori explained. "I'm an assistant in the Arts and Entertainment section. I was trying to make a name for myself by bringing in a report on the new exhibit. The museum was keeping it all such a secret. I thought there had to be something important going on. I wanted to get the story before any other reporter."

"So that's why you were always at the museum asking questions," said Benny.

"I was hoping you kids would tell me something," said Lori. "I listened when you were in the café and made notes in my notebook."

"So that's what you were hiding under the table that day," Henry said.

"I also sneaked up to the exhibit hall a couple of times and tried to peek in," Lori told them.

"We heard your footsteps," Violet said.

"And I did something I regret." Lori looked down at her feet and then back at the children. "One day, I sneaked into the prep room and went through the papers on the desk and looked at the artifacts. I was hoping to learn something to put in the article. But I heard a sound and rushed out before I had a chance to put things back. I'm afraid I left quite a mess."

"What were you doing at the Carson City Museum?" Henry asked.

"I heard they'd tried to get this exhibit, too," said Lori. "So I called them to find out. They wrote to me, and then finally gave me an appointment with the director the day I saw you there."

"And what did she have to say?" Dr. Snood asked.

"She told me at first they were disappointed they hadn't gotten the exhibit," Lori said. "But when she talked with Pete Miller, they came up with some ways the two museums could work together in the future."

"Good work," Dr. Snood told Pete.

"Why were you being so secretive?" Jessie asked Lori.

"I was afraid that if you knew I was a reporter you wouldn't tell me anything," Lori said.

"We thought you were a spy," said Benny.

"A spy?" Lori said. And they all burst out laughing.

"As it turns out," Pete said, "there is quite a story behind this exhibit. And I think the Aldens are just the ones to tell it."

The children spent the rest of the night telling Lori everything that had gone on at the Greenfield Museum while the exhibit was being prepared.

The next morning, Jessie picked up the newspaper at the front door. She brought it in to the kitchen, where the whole family was sitting, eating Mrs. McGregor's special blueberry pancakes for breakfast. Jessie turned straight to the Arts and Entertainment section. There, on the front page, was a picture of the four Aldens standing next to the mummy, and an article written by Lori Paulson, staff reporter. The headline read, ALDEN CHILDREN KEEP MUMMY'S CURSE FROM COMING TRUE.

GERTRUDE CHANDLER WARNER discovered when she was teaching that many readers who like an exciting story could find no books that were both easy and fun to read. She decided to try to meet this need, and her first book, *The Boxcar Children*, quickly proved she had succeeded.

Miss Warner drew on her own experiences to write the mystery. As a child she spent hours watching trains go by on the tracks opposite her family home. She often dreamed about what it would be like to set up housekeeping in a caboose or freight car — the situation the Alden children find themselves in.

When Miss Warner received requests for more adventures involving Henry, Jessie, Violet, and Benny Alden, she began additional stories. In each, she chose a special setting and introduced unusual or eccentric characters who liked the unpredictable.

While the mystery element is central to each of Miss Warner's books, she never thought of them as strictly juvenile mysteries. She liked to stress the Aldens' independence and resourcefulness and their solid New England devotion to using up and making do. The Aldens go about most of their adventures with as little adult supervision as possible — something else that delights young readers.

Miss Warner lived in Putnam, Connecticut, until her death in 1979. During her lifetime, she received hundreds of letters from girls and boys telling her how much they liked her books.